THERE WAS AN OLD LADY WHO SWALLOWED A TURKEY!

by Lucille Colandro
Illustrated by Jared Lee

Cartwheel Books

an imprint of Scholastic Inc.

In memory of Robert Giordano, pie-maker extraordinaire and my first friend.
— L.C.

To Kenja Seuberling, PT.
— J.L.

ISBN 978-0-545-93190-8

10 9   17 18 19 20

Printed in the U.S.A. 40
First printing 2016

There was an old lady who swallowed a turkey.
I don't know why she swallowed the turkey,
but she's always been quirky!

There was an old lady who swallowed a ball.
She stood very tall as she swallowed that ball.

She swallowed the ball to throw with the turkey.
I don't know why she swallowed the turkey,
but she's always been quirky!

There was an old lady who swallowed a hat.
Imagine that! She swallowed a hat.

She swallowed the hat to cover the ball.
She swallowed the ball to throw with the turkey.

I don't know why she swallowed the turkey,
but she's always been quirky!

There was an old lady who swallowed a balloon.

She felt as big as the moon
when she swallowed the balloon!

She swallowed the balloon to bump the hat.
She swallowed the hat to cover the ball.
She swallowed the ball to throw with the turkey.

I don't know why she swallowed the turkey,
but she's always been quirky!

There was an old lady who swallowed a boat.
It slid down her throat when she swallowed that boat.

She swallowed the boat to anchor the balloon.
She swallowed the balloon to bump the hat.
She swallowed the hat to cover the ball.

She swallowed the ball to throw with the turkey.
I don't know why she swallowed the turkey,
but she's always been quirky!

There was an old lady who swallowed some wheels.
She kicked up her heels
when she swallowed those wheels.

She swallowed the wheels to drive the boat.

She swallowed the boat to anchor the balloon.

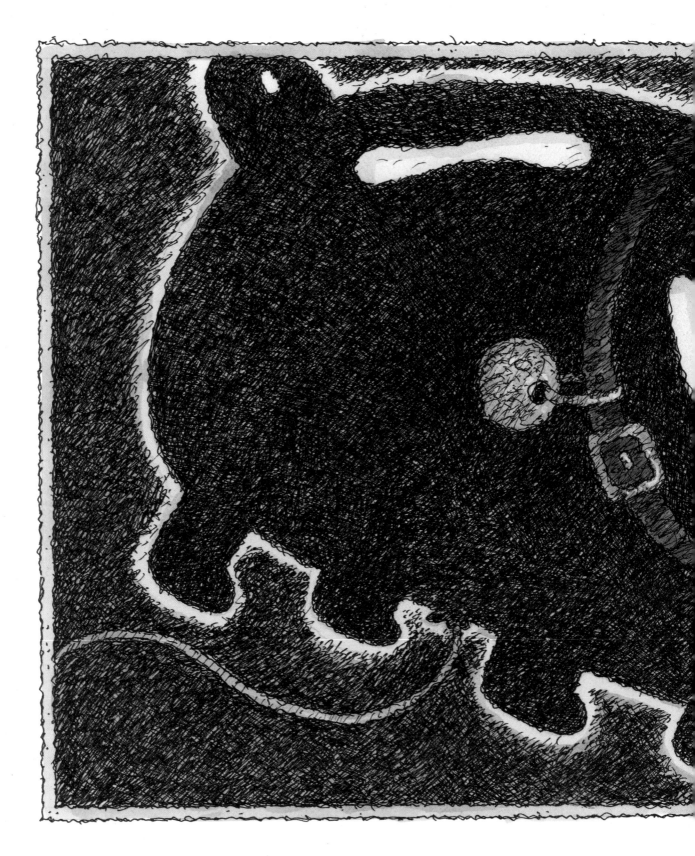

She swallowed the balloon to bump the hat.

She swallowed the hat to cover the ball.

She swallowed the ball to throw with the turkey.

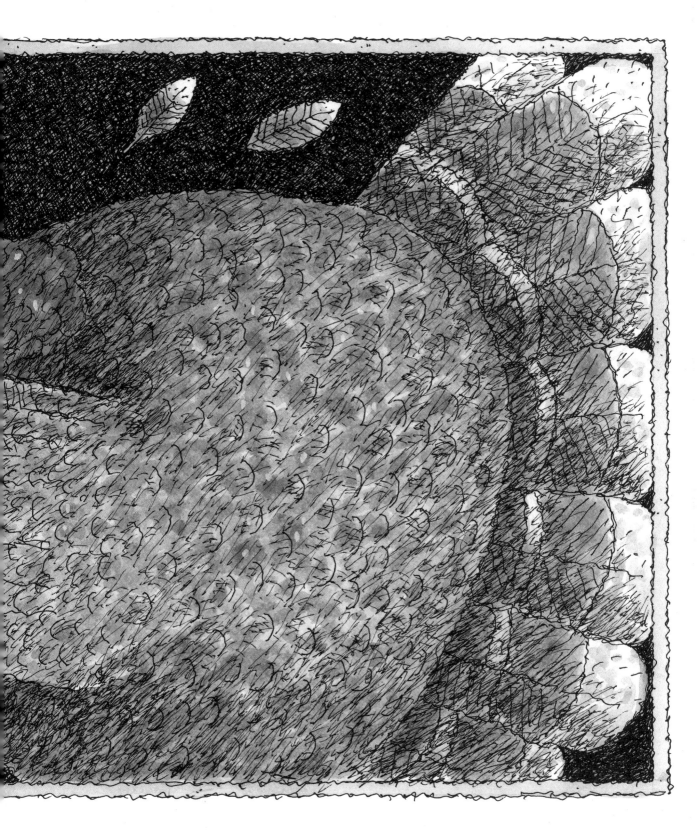

I don't know why she swallowed the turkey,
but she's always been quirky!

There was an old lady who swallowed a horn of plenty.
She could've swallowed twenty horns of plenty.

Just then, the old lady heard a band.
So she marched her way onto the grandstand.

As the parade got under way,
she wished everyone a . . .

Happy Thanksgiving Day!